Published by R. S. Cobb LLC
Printed and distributed by Amazon Kindle Direct Publishing
ISBN: 9798265993823
Cover design by R. S. Cobb
Edited by R. S. Cobb

For permissions, inquiries, or to learn more about the author's work, visit: www.rscobb.com

Printed in the United States of America
First Printing: October 2025
For permissions, please contact:
R. S. Cobb LLC
Ontario, CA 91710
rs_cobb@aol.com

PRELUDE TO BLACKGUARD

ECHOES OF DEFIANCE

As the vibrant village of Icrotvia hummed with life beneath a tapestry of stars in the obsidian sky, hundreds of paper lanterns swayed from weathered oak beams and salt-stained hemp ropes, their flames dancing like imprisoned fireflies. They cast honeyed light across the uneven paths and illuminated the facades of clay brick homes.

Villagers in loose-fitting tunics and dashikis moved through the dusty streets, bartering with traders over baskets of plantains and yams, exchanging hefty amounts of coins for dried fish wrapped in banana leaves. Children with bare feet and sun-browned skin played freely in the shadows of the buildings, darting between the wooden stalls, and pausing only momentarily as Askari patrols in their distinctive blue uniforms passed through the crowded markets.

The hollow thump of skin-stretched drums echoed across the valley, punctuated by bursts of laughter that carried on the night breeze. Smoke from cookfires twisted upward in thin gray ribbons, fragrant with roasting meat and vegetables. Above, a full moon hung like a polished silver coin, casting everything in a blue-white glow.

Moti stood atop a low ridge overlooking the village, his weathered leather cloak swaying in the night breeze. The gentle wind against his skin

I

fueled the calm that had settled into his bones. His son, Mosi, stood beside him. The young man's shoulders were squared, but he shifted from foot to foot, fingers fidgeting with the coins in his pockets. He stood nearly eye-to-eye with his father now, the top of his head just grazing Moti's nose level—sprouting like a young baobab tree over the past year and erasing most of the difference between them.

The moon's silver glow outlined their silhouettes against the night, casting elongated shadows down the jagged ridge. Mosi's eyes were fixed on the flickering fires and moving shapes of the bustling village below, where women prepared evening meals and children chased each other. Moti's mind churned with contradictions—pride in the son who carried his blood, and shame in the violence into which he was born. He found himself filled with dread, not at the boy's coming manhood, but at the path that awaited him.

He's grown… a lot stronger than I was at that age. But what kind of world am I giving back to him? A legacy of violence? A choice I made for him… or was the choice really for my own redemption?

FATE OF FATHERS
PRESENT DAY

As footman Itai and his crew began to haul away the gilded chairs and dismantle the ornate stage of the promotion ceremony, Kuron watched from her room above, which overlooked the sandstone courtyard of Shujaa Pit. The blood-orange sun, sinking behind the western wall, cast long shadows that seemed to match the feelings festering in her heart—remorse that gnawed like termites, guilt that burned like desert sand, shame that clung like a second skin. She looked down at the folded parchment letter, sealed with the emblem of the hyena—its laughing jaws rendered in purple wax. She traced its outline with her thumbnail but could not bring herself to send it off.

She tilted her head slightly as she heard the door to her room open, the hinges betraying the intruder with their familiar creak. A deep breath caught in her lungs, and a moment later, a hand wrapped around her waist, fingers splaying possessively across the fabric of her uniform. The warmth of a strong chest—smelling faintly of cedar and sweat—pressed against her back. Lips brushed the back of her intricate braids with a kiss that lingered just long enough to send a shiver down her spine.

"What is it, love?" Her voice wavered, but she pushed down the ache in her throat. She steadied herself, drawing strength from years of command. The War Chief of Moc Pont had no time for tears. "Tell me, how are your sons?"

Baaku's chest rose with a labored, rattling breath before he answered her. He had changed so much in the past week, becoming nearly unrecognizable. The fight with the Summoned-Akachi had drained most of the vitality from the man Kuron loved. Deep furrows carved valleys across his forehead; his hands, once steady and strong enough to wield large amounts of boko, now trembled like sehfo leaves. Though only in his late thirties, he was withered like an elder who had seen nine decades of harsh desert suns. The wound in his side—a ragged black gash that sent tendrils stretching all the way up his left side to his neck and shoulders—had done more damage than any outcast ever could.

"Ru has regained consciousness, but without aid boko, his leg will take longer to fully heal. The Askari uniform suits Uzoma; he seems ready to be sent on assignment." His gaze drifted to the folded paper clutched in her hand. "You still have Moti's letter, I see."

"Baaku," Kuron said, her voice wavering between accusation and uncertainty. "In all my years as Head Administrator of these training grounds, I have never… I mean, the wena have always been… I protected them. I kept them safe. Then you and your sons arrive, and now… three killed. Three."

"I do apologize for my son's involvement, Kuron," he said as his voice softened.

"I know, Baaku. But you know as well as I do that an apology isn't enough. Maybe if I'd been more vigilant, I could have stopped them from leaving these grounds. I keep thinking about their parents. How do they even begin to… And poor Moti… that man has endured so much already. He trusted me, sent his son here for a better life. The boy died on my watch. I failed him. I failed all of them."

Baaku seized Kuron by the shoulders, his fingers digging into the fabric of her garment as he spun her to face him. Crow's feet radiated from the corners of his eyes like fractured glass. His thick beard, once midnight black, now resembled storm clouds, shot through with silver lightning. The dreads that framed his face hung heavy with ash-colored strands, each one a testament to the wound interfering with his boko. Though time had etched its mark upon him, his presence both filled and commanded the air around them.

She tilted her chin upward, her breath catching as the afternoon light touched his eyes, turning them into amber pools rimmed with honey.

"Do not blame yourself," he leaned forward, his eyes softening at the edges. The tips of his fingers brushed her chin. "You couldn't have known the wena would try to go after Akachi. They were privy to information they shouldn't

have had. It burned like poison in their veins, igniting a reckless arrogance that fueled their misguided bravado. Why have you not sent the letter to Moti?"

She pulled away and walked over to her weapons rack. She ran her finger across the fuller of her ebony blades, lingering at the point where she could feel the edge's threat against her skin. Her mind wandered between the comfort of the familiar blade and the responsibility of what she needed to do.

"Moti could spend the rest of his life in Mateka, never knowing the fate of his son," she said, her voice wavering. "It would be a blessing, wouldn't it? Him, spending his days imagining his son as a great Askari."

"It would be a cruel lie," Baaku said firmly. "In time, he would question why his son never returned to visit him, never wrote to him. That silence would fester into suspicion, that absence gnawing at the soul. He must be allowed to grieve his loss, as Zaiden and Isoke's parents do. The loss of a child is a wound that never heals—an unchosen fate, sudden and merciless, but a fate no father can escape."

She stared down at the folded letter, its seal heavy with finality, then slowly lifted her eyes to Baaku. His hand was waiting—open, steady, and commanding—as though he had plucked the thought straight from her heart before she could shape it into words.

"I'll see that the footman delivers it," he said.

II

ILL-FATED MESSAGE
DAYS LATER

The last rays of the sun bled into the desert sky, and with the emerging stars, the evening air offered a quiet sanctuary from the scorching heat that clung to Askari Acolyte Bakazi's skin. The desert sand stretched and rippled in a sea of gold and shadow, and far in the distance was the shadowed shape of the village of Riliampe. This land was harsh and unforgiving, and his presence here owed solely to his duties as Warden of the Mateka Pits. Yet, over the years, Bakazi had grown to consider this barren, sun-scorched expanse—the Kingdom of Neydow—his own.

He twisted the stopper off his weathered leather drinking-skin and tipped it back, letting the warm mahia pour down his throat. The amber liquid carried the rich sweetness of ripe figs, with a subtle tang that lingered on his tongue and spread a warmth through his chest. He measured each gulp, mindful not to overindulge and dull his senses. Mamman strolled up on his camel next to him. The stout, dark-skinned man's round belly strained against his Askari-blue dashiki. His graying hair receded in the center, leaving a thin crown that gleamed faintly. He held out a hand, and Bakazi passed him the drinking-skin.

"Looks to be another easy night," Mamman said, taking a slow, appreciative swig before returning the skin to Bakazi.

The two of them lingered atop their camels, watching as the sun's last embers guttered out beneath the horizon, surrendering the desert to dusk. A sudden horn blast shattered the stillness, echoing from the stronghold above the

Mateka Pits. Built of pale stone blocks now chipped and worn by centuries of wind and heat, the fortress stood like a weathered sentinel that loomed defiantly over the sands. Above its gate, two banners stirred faintly in the evening breeze— one stamped with the deadly curve of the Cobra, the other painted with the seal of the Askari: a red circle with two spearheads forming an X, with a third driven down the center, blade-first.

Bakazi shifted in his saddle as an Askari bowman atop the stronghold drew his attention, his arm raised and finger pointing southwest. Following the gesture, Bakazi narrowed his gaze on a lone figure who rode steadily toward them.

"I'll intercept," Mamman muttered, spurring his camel toward the approaching figure, but he halted when Bakazi pressed a firm hand against his chest.

"No need."

Summoning his boko into his eyes, Bakazi winced as the sting of the revealing spell burned across his vision. His sight stretched outward, and the world sharpened, every detail alive in impossible clarity. The rider came into focus. He wore a sleek black tunic stitched with silver patterns that ran along the collar and sleeves like veins of moonlight. Bakazi's gaze locked on the silver medallion fastened at the man's collar—twin blades interwoven. He knew it well. The rank of Acolyte.

Through the enchanted sight, the rider's concealment unraveled. Beneath the headwraps lay a square, middle-aged face, framed by close-shorn hair and a neatly trimmed beard. Gold studs winked in both ears, and across his back rested two short spears. Bakazi dismissed his boko, the glow vanishing from his eyes as the ache behind them eased.

"One of ours?" Mamman asked, his fingers tightening around the hilt of the sword at his waist.

"Yes. An Acolyte."

They stood in silence as the lone rider drew nearer, the camel's hooves kicking up plumes of sand with each step. When he finally reined the beast to a halt, the rider straightened and offered the Askari salute— two taps to the left chest with his right hand, and a slight bow—before peeling away his headwraps.

"I am Acolyte Itai, footman of Shujaa Pit," he announced, his voice carrying the weight of duty.

8

"Acolyte Itai," Bakazi returned the salute with practiced ease. "I am Acolyte Bakazi, Warden of Mateka Pits. This is Mamman, my second in command."

Mamman offered his own sharp salute, silent but watchful.

"What drives you to cross into this brutal wasteland?" Bakazi asked, his tone cutting straight to the matter and wasting no time on pleasantries. "Surely, urgent news could have been sent by zirconia."

"True," Itai admitted. From the folds of his garments, he withdrew a carefully folded parchment, the wax seal pressed with the snarling emblem of the Hyena—the sovereign mark of the Kingdom of Moc Pont. "But for a message of this gravity, such means of communication would have been far too impersonal. This comes from War Chief Kuron herself."

"And what news does the War Chief of a neighboring kingdom have for me?" Bakazi asked, his brow tightening with genuine curiosity as he exchanged a glance with Mamman.

"There is much to be discussed," Itai replied, "but this letter is not for you. It is addressed to outcast Moti."

III

DREAD OF SILENCE

Mamman trailed close behind as Acolyte Bakazi guided Acolyte Itai through the sunbaked brick walls of the stronghold. The camels knelt, and the riders slid down, handing their reins to a waiting Askari initiate tasked with tending the stables. Inside, the stronghold's vast courtyard held rows of weapon racks bearing worn swords, splintering spears, and leather quivers filled with frayed arrows. Straw dummies stood scarred, withered, and ripped to shreds from repeated drills. Large hemp targets leaned against stone, pocked with so many arrow impressions their paint was nearly erased.

A narrow stairway climbed to the rampart above, which circled the fortress in a complete ring. Along the walls, Askari blackguards stood with archers and spearmen, their gazes sharp and unwavering, guardians poised to shield Mateka from danger.

"I don't understand," Itai muttered. He turned in a slow circle, his gaze sweeping over the hollow stronghold with its cold, silent walls. "Where are the famed pits I've heard so much about?"

Mamman and the other Askari exchanged knowing looks and let out a low chuckle, their amusement echoing in the emptiness.

"You're standing on them," Mamman said.

Itai trailed close behind Bakazi until they reached two colossal iron doors, their blackened surfaces engraved with the sigil of a cobra, twin gold studs glinting as its eyes. Two Askari swordsmen stood like statues at its threshold, their hands

firm on their hilts. A pungent musk drifted up from the narrow vents in the doors, an odor of sweat and confinement. Of bodies pressed together in suffocating heat.

The two swordsmen slid iron rods into the door handles and heaved. The twin slabs groaned as they were pulled outward, revealing a stairwell of stone that spiraled down into darkness. Smoke hissed upward, dark and acrid, before dissipating into the night.

"Welcome to Mateka Pits," Bakazi said, sweeping a hand toward the dark descent. "Follow me."

The three men pressed downward into the darkened corridor, Mamman bringing up the rear. Rubies infused with the glow of boko pulsed faintly along the cavernous walls. Each gem cast a steady crimson light that pushed back the gloom. When they reached the bottom of the stairwell, two Askari spearmen stood at attention, their posture unshaken as they saluted while the group strode past.

"I never realized the pits stretched beneath the earth like roots beneath the soil," said Itai. "I've lived my whole life in Moc Pont, and spent these past few years serving as Shujaa Pit's head footman. I've rarely strayed far beyond my kingdom's borders. The other kingdoms are a mystery to me."

"Yes," said Bakazi.

As they walked, their footsteps echoed past heavy doors hewn directly into the stone, each one leading deeper into the pits.

"Mateka is more than just a prison," he continued. "It is a labyrinth of caves, carved and expanded over generations. These stone walls have been chiseled, hollowed out, and shaped into various chambers and rooms. This first level serves us, the askari. Here you'll find the dining hall, barracks, library, weapons room, and my own office and quarters. But at the end of this hall lies another stairway—one that carries you down into the bowels of Mateka itself, into the true prison where the outcasts are kept. The cells have been reinforced with steel bars and heavy locks to cage the condemned."

They reached a heavy oak door where a lone Askari initiate stood watch with his spear resting at his side. As the group approached, he snapped a quick salute before resuming his post, shoulders squared like stone. The door itself bore no ornamentation save for the dark emblem of a cobra carved deep into its surface, its fangs bared as though ready to strike. Bakazi slid the key into the lock,

the hinges groaning in protest as the door creaked open. He motioned for Itai to step through first.

"Now then," Bakazi said, holding the letter aloft as he moved behind his desk and eased into his chair, "tell me this news about traitor, Moti."

Mamman, second in command and Bakazi's steadfast protector, remained near the doorway, motionless and watchful. Over the years, Bakazi had become more than a charge—he had become like a son, and Mamman felt the weight of that bond in every guarded breath.

"Moti's son, Mosi, has been killed," Itai's voice faltered as he spoke.

A deafening silence followed, stretching unbearably long, each second punctuated by the weight of loss. Mamman's heart clenched as the boy's face flickered in his memory, a shadow of innocence lost. Bakazi's eyes narrowed, his brow furrowed, and finally, he whispered the question that had been gnawing at him.

"How?"

"It's a long story, and not an easy one," Itai admitted.

Bakazi pulled the leather drinking-skin and retrieved two tarnished metal cups from his desk. He poured the mahia until the liquid sloshed near the brim, then slid one cup across the desk toward Itai. He raised the folded letter and signaled to Mamman, who moved without hesitation, taking it firmly into his grasp.

"Ensure this reaches Moti," Bakazi ordered, eyes narrowing with intensity.

"Yes, sir," Mamman responded, giving the Askari salute before he left the room.

"And take Akli with you. The initiate will benefit from seeing the true depths of the pits firsthand."

Mamman gave a solemn nod and stepped into the corridor, the door whispering shut behind him. He rested his hand on the shoulder of the young Askari who had been keeping watch. The youth tilted his head slightly; his expression caught between puzzlement and intrigue.

"C'mon, youngblood," Mamman said, the sealed parchment clutched firmly in his hand. "Our task awaits, and it won't complete itself."

DEPTHS OF THE PITS

Mamman strode down the corridor with Akli close at his side. The young initiate gripped his spear so tightly his knuckles whitened. Mamman noticed, smirking faintly, even as the foul reek of musk, men, and filth grew heavier with each step deeper into the pits. They had scarcely set foot on the next level when an outcast hurled himself against the bars of his cell, blackened teeth snapping inches from their flesh, desperate to tear into them.

"Damn you, Askari!" the ragged man snarled, his voice cracking like dry wood. Akli leapt back, spear tip trembling toward him.

"Easy, youngblood," Mamman said with a sly grin. "These outcasts are all noise and shadows. They'll hiss and snarl like badgers, but they've got less fight in them than a lemur."

"Right." Akli's voice wavered, his fingers tightening around the shaft of his spear.

The deeper the two of them went, the more the cells came alive with noise. Outcasts screamed and cursed, flinging tin plates and rusted cups with desperate fury that clanged against the.

The women outcast pressed themselves against the iron bars, reaching through the gaps, their voices wet with temptation. Baring skin and whispering promises of release, they offered every pleasure they could give in exchange for freedom. One drew Akli's gaze. Voluptuous and shameless, the full-figured

woman's emerald eyes burned with desire. Her tangled hair tumbled down to her breasts, and the tatters of her dress barely hid what was meant to be concealed. She winked, Akli stiffened and flustered, before he tore his eyes away.

"Careful, youngblood—if you let the little head do the thinking, the big one might end up staring at these bars from the wrong side."

They continued past endless rows of iron-barred cells, their footsteps echoing off the stone walls as they followed a spiraling corridor that wound deeper into the labyrinthine pit. A seemingly endless tier of cells, each row identical to the last. Dim torchlight flickered against the damp stone that curled downward like a coiled serpent. Eventually, they arrived at another stairwell that plunged deeper into the bowels of the pit.

"So, who is this Moti, anyway?" Akli asked, his voice nearly a whisper as they descended. "And why is he important enough to warrant a letter from a War Chief?"

Mamman exhaled through his nose, the question striking deeper than the boy realized. Memories clung to him like cobwebs—Moti's voice in the barracks, his laughter in the training yard, the sharp glint of his illusions. Grief pressed heavily in his chest.

"He was once an Askari," Mamman said at last. "A blackguard of rare skill. With boko, he could twist light itself, bend it until he vanished before your eyes. His illusions fooled even the keenest among us. He became an Acolyte faster than most men dare dream."

They passed another row of cells where shadows of men clawed at the iron bars, their minds splintered from years without daylight. One man murmured incoherent words that hung in the stale air, while another screamed so violently his throat bled with each cracked shout. Akli's steps faltered, his spear wobbling slightly before he forced it steady again.

"So...," his voice faltered. He cleared his throat, then asked, "If he was devoted to the way of the Askari, what could have brought him here?"

"It started with the death of a merchant." Mamman's words slowed, as if dragged from him. His mind was swallowed by memories of the past, of days when his hair was full and his belly flat. He glanced at the boy, then back to the darkness of the pit. His jaw tightened, and his eyes hardened with a grief that never fully left him.

15

CHAINS OF FATE
EIGHTEEN YEARS AGO

Moti moved silently through the market as he slipped into the swelling crowd of the marketplace. At times, he brushed against a shoulder or slipped between bodies in the crowd, but it was explained away as no more than the wind's push or a stranger's passing touch. No one truly noticed him. With his boko woven around him, it blurred his outline, an illusion he had crafted himself two years ago. Invisibility. Of course, if someone were casting a revealing spell, they could pierce the illusion, but they would have to be a blackguard of considerable skill.

Several Askari were already on the scene, struggling to move back the restless crowd from the site of the crime. The people were loud and unruly, voices rising in angry waves.

"Call for a healer!" someone cried out.

"Are any of you blackguards? Do something!" another voice demanded.

"What good is it to join the Askari if your blackguards can't even save a life?" a villager shouted bitterly.

Even as Moti slipped unnoticed through the press of bodies, his eyes caught the dark stains of blood spattered across the ground. As an Acolyte, he had every right to intervene, but caution urged silence until the truth emerged. This marked the third incident in a single week, but the others did not end in bloodshed. A troubling thought whispered—was this the handiwork of *her* trio?

Seh have me! Netsai, you're not making my job easy.

The Askari worked frantically, trying to save an old man whose side was torn by a jagged wound. Their attempts to stem the bleeding were proving futile, and his chest heaved with labored, shallow breaths. Moti knew each of these Askari well: two skilled archers and a seasoned swordsman. But he knew that beyond rudimentary first aid, they lacked the knowledge to keep this man alive.

A deep sense of guilt gnawed at Moti. His talent for illusion was skillful, but his healing skills were clumsy and insufficient, leaving much to be desired.

"Where's Acolyte Moti?" the swordsman called out, eyes scanning the market. "Surely he must have heard the alarm!"

It was already too late. Even if Moti had tried to heal him, the man lay still, his chest no longer rising. An elderly, dark-skinned woman screamed in anguish as she surged from the crowd. She shoved the Askari aside, clutching the fallen man as if to hold him back from death. She cradled him, pressing herself against the lifeless body.

"It was that same group that robbed Kalim!" someone shouted.

"Those three outcasts are always pilfering our wares," another chimed in.

Moti allowed his illusion to vanish, and the crowd collectively gasped as he seemingly appeared from thin air. It took a heartbeat for the three Askari to realize he was there, eyes widening as they finally registered his presence.

"Acolyte, Moti," Ra the archer said, "we did what we could…"

"I know," Moti murmured.

The woman looked up at him, her bloodstained gowns clinging to her, eyes brimming with sorrow, tears streaking her cheeks.

"They must suffer," she said, her jaw tight and voice quaking, anger boiling beneath the tears spilling from her eyes, "just as I have suffered."

The attention of the crowd and the Askari shifted suddenly as a disturbance broke loose. From the mass of bodies burst a short, plump, brown-skin woman, her face red with fury. She barreled forward like a rolling boulder, shoving aside anyone in her path while shrieking curses that cut through the noise of the square. Her eyes locked on the Askari, narrowing at their fixed stares.

After a moment's pause, she raised her chin.

"Well," she announced, "I don't mean to make light of... *this* matter, but someone has stolen items from my cart, and I expect answers from you, Askari."

An older, light-skinned man, perhaps in his forties, with a protruding belly and broad shoulders, shoved his way forward.

"Some goods were stolen from my stall as well," he declared.

"Hey!" another voice shouted. "Half my inventory has been taken!"

A suspicion, sharp as a twisted blade, dug deeper into Moti's gut. If she or her crew were behind not only this killing but also the thefts, he had to know.

Summoning his boko, his eyes burned as the revealing spell improved his sight. He forced his way through the crowd, scanning the plundered stalls one by one. He saw it—the confirmation he dreaded. Regret clenched his chest as wisps of orange boko lingered in the air, spectral traces outlining women who had slipped from cart to cart while the crowd reeled from the murder.

He dismissed his boko, and an almost physical weight seemed to tug at his chest, as if an anchor had fastened itself to his heart.

"Acolyte Moti," Ra said, her voice snapping him back to the moment, "do you see anything that might help us solve this?"

Before Moti could respond, another Askari Acolyte stepped into view. A blackguard he knew all too well, whose eyes were fading from a ghostly green luminescence as the remnants of a revealing spell dissolved.

"Moti," Acolyte Ajamu said. The brown-skinned man, whose neatly trimmed hair framed into a beard that flowed down to his chest, clasped Moti's hand with practiced ease. He, like Moti, wore the Askari's blue dashiki, with embroidered silver swirls curling at its center. The pendant of the Acolyte was pinned to his left collar. "Can I assume you have come to the same conclusion as I?"

Torn by loyalty, Moti had no choice but to answer.

"Yes, Hands," he said. "They murdered this old man to distract the crowd, while another concealed their identity with illusions and seized the opportunity to steal."

"This has gone too far," Ajamu said, his hands curling into a fist, his knuckles tight with restrained anger.

"I agree," Moti replied, though it was not duty that compelled him, but his love for Netsai that stirred his resolve.

"A bounty must be placed on their heads," Ajamu said, his voice sharp. "One silver coin each. I will present it to War Chief Gamba so he may decree it. Or... would you like to present it?"

Suddenly, the world tilted. Moti's legs turned to liquid beneath him, threatening to collapse at any moment.

"I cannot," he admitted, breath shallow. "The day has been long, and I am spent. But give me a copy once it's set."

Moti had made up his mind. His next move was already taking shape in his thoughts. He needed to protect her without exposing the forbidden truth—that his loyalty to the Askari had been broken by love through their illicit affair. He would show her the bounty for her life, giving her a chance to flee without any harm befalling her. Her friends, however, would pay with their lives for killing the old man.

DEEPER THEY GO
PRESENT DAY

Mamman and Akli pressed deeper into the pits, where the wails of the outcast dwindled, swallowed by the relentless clang of metal on stone and the grunt of laboring men. The wall-mounted flame torches, this deep into the pits, were few and scattered. To break the gloom, Mamman drew out a small torch fashioned from a hollowed goat horn and set its flame alight with a match. The dim glow guided their path forward.

The cavern walls were a deep, obsidian black, yet they resonated with an eerie presence. Iridescent minerals fractured and scattered the dim torchlight, breaking into prismatic glimmers that danced across the darkness.

"Is that amanzara?" Akli asked, narrowing his eyes to examine it. The moment his eyes focused, he winced and recoiled sharply.

"Best not to gaze directly into it, youngblood," Mamman cautioned, tugging the initiate back. "Stare too long, and it'll burn your eyes blind."

Mamaman and Akli came upon a shadowed corridor guarded by two Askari spearmen. The air thickened with the sounds of men straining at their toil. Curses flung at both Askari and fellow prisoners, mixed with grunts and the harsh ring of stone being chipped.

"Who goes there?" one of the spearmen demanded, thrusting out his arm to halt their approach. The dim torchlight caught the edge of his spear, casting long shadows on the rough, stone wall.

"At ease," Mamman said, his voice steady. He raised the folded letter so the spearman could clearly see it. "It's me—Mamman. I carry a message for the outcast, Moti."

"And what's he doing with you?" the second spearman asked, eyeing Akli. "Initiates aren't permitted this deep into the pits."

"Because Acolyte Bakazi commanded it," Mamman answered, his tone edged with impatience. "Now, will you let an old man through, or must I limp all the way back up and inform the Acolyte that you two prevented me from carrying out his orders?"

The first spearman lowered his guard. "Very well. But tread carefully. Some of the new tunnels the prisoners are burrowing haven't been reinforced yet and are already starting to collapse."

"And the floor is littered with rubble," the other added. "Watch your footing."

Mamman gave the two warriors a crisp Askari salute and strode past them, Akli shadowing his every step.

Bound in thick, unforgiving chains, outcasts—old and young, weak and strong, male and female—hammered into stone with brutal rhythm. Their pickaxes and shovels slammed against the cave walls, their labor relentless. Askari spearmen observed silently, prodding anyone who faltered with the cold points of their spears.

"No rest for the wicked down here," Mamman said, his voice carrying over the echoing strikes.

Akli didn't respond, swallowing down the rising tide of pity that threatened to make him vomit. The cells on this level were far tighter than those above. Their grimy walls were slick with an unexplained dampness. It left a sour tang in the air that was oppressive and foul.

The outcasts cast them scornful glances as they passed. One of them, a young male not yet fully grown, lifted his head and caught Akli's gaze. He held it with a bold, chilling defiance.

"Were it not for these walls, my boko would tear your flesh from your bones, and your skull would join my collection."

Akli said nothing to the outcast, his gaze shifting instead to Mamman, who was steadily pulling ahead through the shadows. The older man moved unfazed by the threats.

"So… it's true," Akli murmured, falling into step just behind Mamman, "that amanzara can nullify boko?"

"Yes," Mamman said, leading them down a cramped, shadowed corridor. "It's why we confine the more dangerous outcasts to these lower levels—skull hunters, outcast blackguards, and the like. These depths are heavily guarded, making escape far more difficult."

An Askari spearman on patrol nodded to them as they passed, his gaze brief but watchful.

"It must take a lot of effort and real skill to capture these outcasts, right?" Akli asked.

"More than you might imagine," Mamman admitted.

"Then how did this Moti end up here?"

Mamman paused, turning to face Akli. Darkness clung to them like a suffocating shroud, broken only by the faint glow of his torch.

"A woman was his undoing," he said quietly. "He fell in love with an outcast."

STAR-CROSSED
TWENTY YEARS AGO

Leaves and branches whipped across Moti's face as he tore through the jungle, his body surging with the amplified fury of his boko. Each breath seared his lungs, thick with the musk of the damp night air. He pressed on, his stride carried the predatory strength of a jaguar. Ahead, the outcast darted from branch to branch like a phantom, always just beyond reach, weaving through the labyrinth of towering mahogany trees.

He knew this was his only chance to stop the thief. His muscles trembled, on the verge of failing beneath the strain of his boko, yet he drew the force into his palm. A condensed orb of orange energy whirled within his fingers, like a storm. Fixing his gaze on the fleeing figure, he summoned all his strength and unleashed the blast in a blinding eruption.

It hissed like a viper as it tore through the air with blistering speed—not at the intended target, but at the branch she had sprung toward. With a crack like thunder, the limb exploded in a burst of wood chips and searing orange light, dropping her from above. She hit the ground hard but flowed seamlessly into a roll, her movements quick and practiced, until she slid into a crouch.

When she lifted her gaze, her luminous brown eyes caught the moonlight. They glimmered back at him with both defiance and beauty. A gaze of quiet intensity that was as breathtaking as it was dangerous.

With a final burst of enhanced reflexes, he lunged toward her. His hands grasped for her shoulders, only to pass through as if she were mist. He struck the

ground with bone-jarring force, scattering dirt and brittle leaves in every direction. He rolled on his side with a pained groan, every movement pulling fire through his battered body.

As her illusion unraveled into a wisp of orange light, fading like smoke on the wind, the true assailant lunged. A blade kissed his throat—cold, jagged, and rusted. Instinct drove him to summon his boko, but before the thought could become movement, the ground betrayed him. Roots erupted like glowing orange serpents, snaring his arms and legs, locking him in a prison of living wood.

"You'll have to do better than that, Askari," she murmured, leaning so close that her breath brushed against his lips. He was utterly at her mercy. Her voice, steady yet laced with mockery, cut sharper than any blade.

Yet, it was her eyes that held him captive. Deep brown, rimmed with an auburn fire, they stole the breath from his chest. He could not look away. Not from the dagger pressed to his throat, not from the capture spell that pinned him helplessly, but from her—only her.

"Netsai!" a voice rang through the dense trees.

She glanced toward the forest, pausing just long enough for him to glimpse the unspoken thought behind her gaze. She lifted her blade, and the spell uncoiled from his limbs. Step by careful step, she began to back away, slowly and deliberately.

"Next time," she said, a sharp undertone within her calm, "I won't be so forgiving."

And just like that, she vanished, her figure dissolving into the dense, shadowed embrace of the forest.

In the Kingdom of Sonarc, south of the village of Icrotvia, a vast lake stretched toward the eastern ocean. There, under the quiet hum of cicadas, Moti spotted her again. Moonlight danced across the rippling water as she lathered black soap over her skin, running her fingers through her hair. Wet strands cascaded down her back, revealing the soft contours of her face.

He paused, measuring his approach, silently summoning his boko to test his latest illusion. After their last encounter, he had spent the entire week devoted to mastering this spell. Channeling his boko throughout his body, he concentrated

on weaving the surrounding light around him—bending it to conceal his form. He cloaked his presence in perfect invisibility.

The strain hit him instantly. His mind and muscles screaming in protest. Every second counted as he had only minutes to capture her before dispelling his boko.

He entered the lake unnoticed, the cool water rising around him as his eyes traced the way it clung to her skin, outlining her curves in glimmering silver moonlight. She turned as if she had known he was there all along but appeared not to notice him. He paused a short distance away. Her gaze swept across the lake, though she hadn't seen him. Her lips, full, wet, and inviting, curved into a smile that was both amusement and challenge.

Without a moment's hesitation, he lunged, his boko dissipating as his hand clamped down on her shoulder. Her body dissolved into a swirling cloud of orange smoke—another illusion. The water quivered where she had been, rippling as the smoke spiraled downward into the lake below. He leaned closer, scanning the depths, and noticed a soft, eerie glow returning his gaze. He plunged his hand into the water and pulled out a zirconia, its core throbbing with pulsating orange boko.

"Why do you keep chasing me, Askari?" she asked from just behind him, "if you never intend to catch me?"

He drew in a slow, deliberate breath, turning to face her. There she was—small but deadly—a slender blade aimed at him in one hand, boko thrumming with intent in the other. He should have feigned allegiance to duty, honor, or authority. But in the soft, silver light of the moon, her eyes, her lips, the curve of her form, her very presence… all of it called to him.

"Because I want you," the truth surged out, raw and unstoppable, breaking through like a dam. His voice faltered, heavy with longing. "From the moment I first saw you, I've yearned for you. Pursuing you became the only path back to you. And I swear, I will chase you… forever."

The night was hushed, the only sound the rhythmic pulse of his own heartbeat. Even the cicadas had fallen silent. For a long moment, she simply watched him, the moonlight shimmering in her eyes. Then, slowly, her boko dissipated, she lowered her weapon, and she advanced a step toward him.

"And if I told you I feel the same?" she murmured, her voice drifting like the gentle sehha breeze.

He acted before thought could intervene. Their lips met— fierce, hungry, desperate. The outcast and the Askari, tethered by a fire neither could quench. Within the lake's glassy expanse, beneath a tapestry of stars, they surrendered to every craving. To the danger. To the betrayal. To the love that would damn them both.

WHEN BRAVADO FAILED
PRESENT DAY

Bakazi tipped back his cup and gulped down more mahia, wiping the trickle slipping down his lip with the back of his hand before refilling. Disbelief clung to him like a fog after hearing Itai's words. Out of habit, he reached to top off Itai's drink, but the man waved him off, his first drink still untouched.

"So," Bakazi began slowly, "this Akachi was nothing but an illusion?"

Itai inclined his head. "Perhaps he lived once, but the one who stood in Swindler's Den was not mortal. He was a summoned construct, a spirit reshaped by boko into Akachi's likeness."

Bakazi nodded, struggling to reconcile what he heard, both shaken and perplexed.

"I have never heard of boko being twisted to such a purpose."

"Well," Itai said, raising his empty cup in request before setting it down, "Baaku and his sons claim that Amadi's boko had been corrupted."

Bakazi poured the amber liquor with a slow nod. *Corrupted boko*—the bane of every Blackguard, Askar, and outcast alike. It was a possession of the mind, a poison that rewrote desire into obsession. Such corruption could warp a person's very thoughts and emotions until they were no longer their own. It promised immense power beyond measure, but always at the steepest cost: sanity. Once corruption took hold, the Blackguard was no longer the master. The boko was.

"What a cruel fate for one so young to bear," Bakazi murmured, shaking his head in disbelief. He drew in a slow, steadying breath, as though the weight of the boy's suffering pressed on his own chest. "Amadi's life must have been nothing but hardship upon hardship."

"Indeed," Itai replied, lifting the cup of mahia to his lips before continuing. "Baaku's sons told us that when they arrived at Swindler's Den, the Summon-Akachi struck swiftly, cutting down three of the wena without hesitation. Among the dead was Mosi—Moti's own son."

Bakazi's fist crashed against the desk, and he pushed back his chair. He began to pace in agitation, grief giving way to simmering frustration.

"What madness drove them to make such a reckless decision? Confronting a rumored outcast of such power? That isn't bravado; it's blind ignorance."

"Elite Baaku's sons are fortunate to have survived," Itai remarked.

"And you would have me believe this Summon-Akachi killed not only War Chief Anaan but War Chief Sandile as well?"

"And countless more Askari are among the fallen and wounded as well. The village of Llma in the Kingdom of Roctrane was devastated, though recovery efforts are already underway. Word of these events has been dispatched to the other kingdoms and remaining War Chiefs—even to the War Lord himself." Itai sat back in his studying the younger Acolyte with quiet intensity.

Bakazi's mind churned. Wena sneaking out of the Shujaa Pit, the taint of corrupted boko, the death of so many of his brethren, that monstrous entity conjured into being. Each thought struck like a hammer. A question formed in his mind like a spark catching flame.

"If the Summon-Akachi possessed such overwhelming strength, how could Elite Baaku have possibly defeated it?"

"Defeated might not be the right word," Itai admitted

"What do you mean?"

"In the midst of the battle, his son, Uzoma, unleashed a beam that struck Amadi, killing him outright. With his death, the summon vanished, its form fading into nothing."

Bakazi sank heavily into his chair and chugged the mahia from its skin until the bag was bone dry. He tossed it aside and pulled out another, full, brimming, and tempting, yet he only stared at it before returning it to its place.

"Seh have me, Itai… I never expected such dreadful news to cross these sands," he murmured after a pause. "And Moti… he trusted the Askari to protect his son, to bring him into our ranks—only for the young Wena to be led straight to his slaughter. I may not have the blessing of fatherhood, but when he reads that letter, I know… his heartbreak will be unbearable."

A FATHER'S SACRIFICE
SIX MONTHS AGO

Rolling hills stretched endlessly before them, a living ocean of green spilling into the horizon. Mamman strode in step with Lubanzi and Acolyte Bakazi, their unit moving in tight formation as they escorted Moti and his son, Mosi, toward Shujaa Pit. Trees blanketed the slopes, their branches draped with vines of pink and white blossoms. Meerkats darted playfully among the rocks while hummingbirds shimmered through the air, sipping nectar from blossom to blossom.

The clatter of chains followed Moti with every step, the iron around his neck, wrists, and ankles rattling like a grim chorus. Shards of amanzara embedded in the manacles pulsed with faint menace. Bakazi trailed just far enough back to avoid their dampening effect on his boko, yet close enough to strike if Moti made a move. Mamman, however, suspected no such defiance would come.

Since leaving Mateka Pits seven days earlier, father and son had not exchanged a single word, their silence as heavy as the chains themselves. Mosi strode briskly at the head of the group, his posture tall and unyielding, chin lifted in quiet defiance despite the weight of the circumstances.

As their destination drew near, the road thickened with recruits. Youth from every corner of the eight kingdoms of Sol Galnese made their way to the Shujaa Pit at this time of year. Some arrived in carriages draped in silks, others rode atop camels or striped zebras, while many came trudging on foot, dust clinging to their ankles. Families came with them—stern fathers, watchful

mothers, uncles brimming with advice, elders speaking blessings, and Askari relatives whose presence lent both weight and warning. The wealthier families cast sidelong looks of disdain as they passed Moti, but his face betrayed nothing—stone-like, hardened by fatigue, unreadable as ever.

Every so often, sunlight refracted off the amanzara set into the chains, forcing Mamman to avert his gaze. Out of the corner of his eye, he noticed Mosi had drawn the wary attention of a young boy in a nearby carriage, who stared at him with quiet unease.

The colossal walls of Shujaa Pit loomed higher with every step, stretching skyward with an unyielding presence. Archers and blackguards lined the battlements with watchful eyes, poised to strike at any would-be offenders. At the center above the towering gates stood a lone figure, distant yet commanding. Mamman's gut told him this was War Chief Kuron. Though he had never met her before, tales of her ebony blades cutting down outcasts had reached him, each story sharper than the steel itself.

Mamman looked to Moti, his bound wrists stretched tight as he strained against the chains that bound him to his fate. A lone tear welled in his eye before falling, disappearing into the ground.

A horn bellowed across the landscape, halting the five men in their tracks. The sound was long and unyielding, echoing farther than any cry could reach, commanding the air itself. The crowd of hundreds of people waited just yards away from the colossal gates of Shujaa Pit. The gates rose nearly ten yards high, forged from enormous wooden stumps lashed tightly together, their jagged, sharpened tips jutting upward like a crown of spears.

Kuron blew her horn once more, its deep, resonant tone carrying across the land, calling all the travelers to attention. "Welcome to Shujaa Pit," she announced.

A third, commanding blast of the horn followed, and the massive gates groaned as they began to open, inviting the recruits inside. Mamman hadn't laid eyes on these gates in more than fifty years, and the sight stirred a flood of memories from his youth as a young wena.

With his back turned, Mosi looked over his shoulder and offered a quiet, deliberate nod. Moti remained stiff, his features set and unyielding, yet he nodded in return. As Mosi strode toward the open gates of Shujaa Pit, Bakazi signaled Mamman and Lubanzi to begin escorting Moti away.

The outcast didn't budge, lingering for a heartbeat longer—an echo of defiance etched into his breath.

"I love you!" Moti yelled.

IIII IIII

THE COLDESLT DEPTHS
PRESENT DAY

Torchlight from the flame post outside flickered across the cavern walls, casting shadows that writhed like restless spirits as the chill drafts slid through his cell. The amanzara walls bent and refracted the glow, turning the darkness into a shifting prism of haunting brilliance. How long had it been? How many months had passed? How many days? Still no word from Mosi.

I In the bowels of the Mateka Pits, time stretched endlessly. For Moti, some days were more suffocating than others—but he marked them all, no matter how heavy the burden. A tally etched into the stone.

The promotion ceremony must have ended by now. Surely his son would visit him before leaving on assignment—or would Bakazi steal even that solace from him? It was torment enough to be hemmed in by amanzara, its very presence severing his bond with the benign. Day after day, he clawed for some trace of his boko, desperate to grasp even the faintest thread. He hurled his will against the silence, summoned it with every fiber of his being, but nothing stirred. It was as if a limb had gone numb, a part of him lost, unresponsive, and useless.

He sat on the cold stone bench inside his cell, which was little more than a hollowed-out cave sealed by iron bars. Drawing in a slow, deliberate breath, he fought back the pull of his darkest thoughts.

Another day… another day without him.

Moti's decision to turn himself in left his son feeling betrayed, yet he knew it was the only path that could safeguard his son's future. The boy deserved—if nothing else—the opportunity to strive for an ordinary life beyond the shadows of his father's choices. He would understand one day.

Moti reached for the sharp fragment of ivory lying at his side on the bench. The splintered bone had become his only measure of time. He ran his eyes over the wall scarred with dozens of tallies, located the newest group of four, and scored a diagonal line across them. When he finished, faint footsteps and the muffled voices of two Askari drifted down the cavern passage. Moti recognized one of the voices—it was Mamman. But what was he doing so far down in these dark depths?

When they stopped just beyond the bars of his cell, he tightened his grip on the bone, staring at it in silence.

"Moti," Mamman said, his voice thick with hesitation. "I have news about your son."

THE END

THE ASKARI LEXICON

RANKINGS OF THE ASKARI

War Lord–The War Lord is the esteemed leader of the Askari, holding the highest rank among their ranks. Answering solely to the King and Queen of Sol Galnese, the War Lord plays a pivotal role in maintaining peace and harmony between the eight kingdoms. They accomplish this by hand-picking Elites and nominating War Chiefs, who are entrusted with overseeing the well-being of their respective kingdoms. Through strategic assignments, the War Lord ensures the presence of Askari in key positions throughout the realm.

Wraith–The rank of Wraith is a highly exclusive distinction granted to only a select few Askari. The sole authority to choose individuals for this esteemed rank lies with the War Lord. Wraiths are entrusted with the exceptional responsibility of operating beyond the confines of the law when necessary to prevent crimes or apprehend outcasts. Their unique status grants them the autonomy to employ unconventional methods in fulfilling their duties. Although they may collaborate with War Chiefs and Elites, Wraiths answer to neither, possessing a level of independence that sets them apart within the Askari ranks.

War Chief–A position of great responsibility, War Chiefs are nominated by the War Lord and must receive the approval of the Chieftain in the kingdom they will serve. Operating in close collaboration with the Chieftain, War Chiefs manage the intricate affairs of individual villages within their assigned kingdom. They hold the authority to appoint Acolytes and other Askari to specific posts, ensuring the smooth functioning of the Askari forces and the prosperity of their designated territories.

Elite–The coveted rank of Elite is bestowed upon revered and battle-hardened warriors among the Askari. Tasked with being the first line of defense against outcasts and wrongdoers, Elites are formidable fighters and exemplify the pinnacle of Askari prowess. While answerable to War Chiefs, Elites enjoy considerable autonomy and possess the freedom to investigate and operate within any part of the kingdom they reside. This rank serves as an aspiration for many Askari, and promotion to Elite can only be granted by another Elite or a War Chief, reflecting the esteemed status it holds.

Acolyte—Acolytes are full-fledged Askari who have achieved mastery in their chosen classification, a process that often takes several years of rigorous training and dedication. Promotion to the rank of Acolyte is only granted by the War Chief, but it comes with the condition that the Askari must indisputably prove their mastery in one of the four classifications. Acolytes hold the responsibility of leading small companies of Askari, further honing their leadership skills and guiding their fellow warriors with wisdom and expertise.

Full-Fledged—Not an actual rank, an Askari denoted as Full-Fledged marks a significant milestone in an Askari's journey. It is bestowed upon those who have served in their post for over a year and have proven their dedication and commitment to the Askari cause. No longer considered initiates, Full-Fledged Askari have gained valuable experience, honed their skills, and proven their loyalty. This achievement signifies their transition from a novice to a seasoned member of the Askari, ready to take on greater responsibilities and contribute to the defense and well-being of their village and kingdom.

Initiate – Not an actual rank, an Askari denoted as initiate signifies a wena who has recently been promoted to the Askari ranks. After undergoing intensive training in the prestigious Shujaa Pit, these young adults have proven their commitment and potential to serve as Askari warriors. As Initiates, they embark on a path of continuous growth, building upon their foundational training to further develop their skills, discipline, and understanding of the Askari principles. Guided by experienced mentors and immersed in the traditions of the order, Initiates embrace their role with determination, aspiring to ascend through the ranks and fulfill their duty as defenders of their people.

Wena - A wena represents a young adult chosen and sent to the renowned Shujaa Pit for training to become an Askari. These individuals demonstrate promise, resilience, and a sense of responsibility, making them worthy candidates for the rigorous

instruction and transformative experiences that await them in the training grounds. Immersed in the teachings of the Askari, wenas undergo comprehensive physical and mental conditioning, learn combat techniques, and develop their character, embodying the virtues and values that define the noble order. With each passing day in Shujaa Pit, they inch closer to realizing their potential as future guardians.

ASKARI CLASSIFICATIONS

Swordman – These Askari warriors possess unparalleled skill and expertise in wielding bladed weapons, making them invaluable assets on the battlefield. As masters of the sword, they are entrusted with the defense and honor of their kingdom.

Spearman – With their mastery of staff weapons, Spearman Askari are the guardians of the front lines. Their agility and precision in combat make them formidable adversaries, striking with deadly accuracy and defending their comrades with unwavering determination.

Bowman – Masters of long-range warfare, Bowman Askari are known for their unrivaled proficiency with bows, crossbows, and other ranged weapons. They unleash volleys of arrows with unparalleled precision, decimating enemies from a distance and maintaining dominance over the battlefield.

Blackguard – Distinguished by their exceptional proficiency in harnessing the mystical essence known as boko. Blackguards use boko to cast powerful spells, granting them unparalleled advantages both on and off the battlefield.

OUTCAST

In the country of Sol Galnese, outcasts come in various forms, each with their own motivations and levels of danger. Here are some expanded details about each type:

Common Outcast - Common outcasts are individuals who have become enemies of the people of Sol Galnese and are involved in criminal activities. While they may operate in groups, the most common outcasts are low-level criminals. They pose a continuous threat to the safety and well-being of the general population. To combat this menace, the Askari are responsible for apprehending or eliminating these dangerous individuals. In certain cases, when an outcast becomes exceptionally dangerous or poses a significant threat, the War Chiefs of the different Kingdoms have the authority to place bounties on their heads, incentivizing their capture or demise.

Outcast Blackguard - An outcast blackguard is a blackguard who utilizes their boko for personal gain, power, or influence, but without adhering to the established guidelines. To wield boko, one must either be an Askari or be in the service of their kingdom. Outcast blackguards disregard these requirements and use their powers for their own purposes, making them outcasts in the eyes of society. These individuals often seek to exploit their abilities, seeking wealth, dominance, or control over others, which puts them at odds with both the law and the established order.

Skull-Hunters - Skull-hunters represent a particularly vile and feared faction of outcasts. They are known for adorning the skulls of their victims around their necks like a macabre necklace, a symbol of their gruesome accomplishments. Skull-hunters usually travel in groups and are comprised of fierce fighters, often including blackguards among their ranks. They actively recruit other outcasts, enticing them to join their cause and fill the ranks of their group. When an outcast under their tutelage achieves their first kill, they are given the title of "**skull-wearer,**" marking their initiation. As they accumulate more kills, reaching a threshold of three, they earn the title of "full-fledged skull-hunter," solidifying their status as a lethal force to be reckoned with.

BOKO

Boko manifests as a vibrant and swirling aura, emanating from the blackguard's palms. The color of the boko corresponds to the blackguard's specific mental and emotional state of being. The pulsations of boko are dynamic and will fluctuate in intensity and speed depending on the blackguard's emotions, intentions, or the level of power they are exerting. Their boko might crackle, surge, or even emit sparks, representing the raw power and potential within the blackguard.

BOKO SPELLS

A **Barrier Spell** protects with a shield of boko energy, defending against harm. Blackguards concentrate their boko, shaping it into a solid shield that deflects attacks, safeguarding their bodies from harm in battles. The barrier shields against physical attacks, spells, and hostile forces, its strength based on the blackguard's skill and energy. Blackguards extend the barrier over individuals or groups, ensuring safety and mobility.

An **Afterimage Spell** can be used to confuse and deceive enemies. Concentrating on gathering boko within themselves, blackguards visualize the desired afterimage, radiating a pulsating aura. Releasing the boko in a burst, the afterimage manifests, mimicking the blackguard's movements. Serving as a decoy, it forces the enemy to split their attention, allowing the blackguard to exploit openings and gain an upper hand. Although temporary, the afterimage provides strategic advantages in battles, aiding the blackguard in overcoming formidable opponents.

Illusion Spells can trap and manipulate an enemy's perception. Through their boko, they form vivid illusions that deceive and confuse foes. These illusions encompass visual and auditory deception, creating a convincing and immersive experience. Blackguards can deceive opponents with illusions of overwhelming force or hazardous surroundings. Their boko abilities make them formidable opponents, capable of turning the tide of battle through manipulation and deception.

A **Levitation Spell** is a concentration of boko on a desired object to manipulate its gravity and lift the object. The blackguard's control over boko determines the lifting capacity, allowing them to increase levitation force gradually. To sustain levitation, they must continuously infuse the object with boko while countering external disturbances. The blackguard's strength and skill affect the weight limit of the objects they can effortlessly lift. Levitation spells demand mental focus and a strong connection to boko, making them physically and mentally demanding.

The **Craft Weapon Spell** is a powerful technique used by blackguards to summon weapons by manipulating matter or focusing their boko. To cast the spell, the blackguard must visualize the desired weapon. Matter or boko gathers and compresses around their hand, taking shape. These conjured weapons are versatile and durable, capable of causing significant damage. However, their lifespan depends on the blackguard's concentration.

A *Capture Spell* restrains any enemy. By infusing chosen objects with boko, they will bind and restrict their adversary's movements. The blackguard focuses their boko on various objects like ropes, chains, or ethereal tendrils. These objects pulsate with an ethereal glow and possess supernatural strength, ensnaring the target effectively. The charged objects are unleashed towards the opponent, adapting their form to secure a grip. Once captured, the objects will tighten around the opponent, making escape difficult.

The *Summoned-Weapons Spell* is a powerful technique used by blackguards to summon lethal weapons made of boko energy that swiftly assault their adversaries. To start the spell, the blackguard channels their boko energy, creating an electrified atmosphere and a shimmering aura. The number and types of weapons summoned depend on the blackguard's skill and strategic assessment. Once materialized, the blackguard controls the weapons with precision, directing them to strike their targets with lethal force.

Through a *Summoning Spell*, Blackguards possess the power to conjure creatures from other realms. Through their mastery of boko and connection to otherworldly planes, they channel energy to call forth specific creatures. These summoned entities materialize in various forms, such as warriors, beasts, or elemental forces. Bound to the blackguard's will, they fight with loyalty and skill. Although resilient, the creatures can be dispelled under certain conditions: if the blackguard's boko depletes, if the blackguard dies, or if the summoned creature returns to its realm.

The *Blasting Spell* is used when blackguards summon boko and unleash it as destructive concussive blasts. To perform the spell, blackguards tap into their boko, converging it into their hands. As the energy intensifies, their palms emit a radiant glow, indicating the spell's gathering power. With focused concentration, blackguards release the amassed energy, propelling it forward as a blast. The blast carries immense force, shattering objects and leaving destruction in its wake. Experienced blackguards exhibit even greater control, maximizing destructive potential while exercising caution and precision.

The *Revealing Spell* enhances a blackguard's vision tenfold by infusing boko directly into their eyes. With deep concentration, the blackguard channels boko energy towards their eyes, creating a connection between the energy and their vision. As the energy flows, their irises emit a subtle yet powerful glow, showing the spell's activation and improved vision. Colors become vibrant, details

sharpen, and even the finest nuances become clear. However, this comes at a cost, as the longer the spell remains active, the more strain it puts on their eyes.

The **Beam Spell** is a powerful technique used by blackguards by channeling boko into their forefingers, then releasing it as a concentrated beam. The accumulated energy is radiant, crackles with power, and can pierce through most materials. However, inexperienced blackguards must be cautious, as mishandling this spell can lead to injuries like burns or fractures.

The **Healing Spell** harnesses boko, accelerating natural healing and promoting recovery. By focusing, blackguards initiate the spell with a touch or a hovering palm. A soothing aura of light envelops the injured, blending boko energy with life force to facilitate healing. The energy stimulates cell regeneration and repairs damaged tissues swiftly and efficiently. Superficial wounds vanish while deeper ones gradually close. While effective for physical injuries, its power varies depending on severity, proficiency, and the blackguard's skill with boko.

The **Enhancement Spell** boosts strength, speed, and agility. By tapping into their boko, blackguards amplify their physical abilities. They focus and let boko flow through their muscles. The spell empowers them, making them stronger, faster, and more agile. However, the strain takes a toll, leaving them drained and fatigued after deactivation.

BOKO GEM INFUSION

A **Zirconia** infused with boko can store and project memories or messages. By focusing boko, a blackguard imprints desired memories or crafts a message. The infused zirconia emits a faint glow, shimmering with an ethereal luminescence. Activated with boko energy, the zirconia levitates, projecting a holographic message or memories. The holographic projection vividly displays visuals and scenes, immersing the recipient in the imprinted information. Once the projection ends, the zirconia descends, and its glow fades.

A **Ruby** infused with boko emits light and heat like a flame. To infuse the ruby, a blackguard concentrates, directs their boko into the gemstone. The ruby gemstone glows brightly, becoming a radiant source, casting a mesmerizing glow, and emitting warmth. When the blackguard withdraws their boko, the ruby returns to its unassuming form.

Sapphires infused with boko energy can deploy motion when attached to carriages and carts. Concentrating on the gemstones, blackguards send their boko into them. The sapphires emit a pulsating blue aura and an ethereal glow. Once infused, the wheels are propelled with remarkable speed and grace. Blackguards control the vehicle's movements using their attuned boko. Withdrawing boko energy returns the sapphires and vehicle to their inert state.

An *Iolite Crystal* infused with boko stores healing energy for later healing. The blackguard taps into their boko, channeling it through their body and hands to focus on healing. The iolite crystal acts as a conduit, amplifying the blackguard's energy. The energy merges with the crystal, creating a harmonious resonance. The stored energy can then be directed towards the recipient for healing, tailored to their needs.

POTIONS & REMEDIES

A *Healing Remedy* is a green substance contained in a glass phial. It is made from medicinal herbs burned with a healing spell until liquified. The remedy is typically available in Tesriaa and is used to soothe aches, pains, and revitalize the body. The remedy is consumed by drinking the liquid. It has a taste reminiscent of seawater and provides a cooling effect.

CORRUPTED BOKO

When a blackguard has corrupted boko, it infiltrates the mind, and the consequences are harrowing and awe-inspiring. Blackguards succumb to its influence, plagued by distorted thoughts and emotions. Connected to the cesspool, corrupted boko grants unparalleled power, but it corrodes sanity, causing erratic behavior and disregard for others.

BOKO GAMUT

BOKO	PERSONALITY/EMOTIONS
White	Devoid: Corrupted Mind, Empty, Indifferent
Red	Passionate: Anger, Disdain, Vindictive, Hatred
Orange	Lust: Desire, Greed, Aggravated, Aggression, Anxious
Yellow	Pride: Ambition, Diligent, Debauchery, Belligerent
Green	Happy: Naïve, Hopeful, Willing, Trustful, Tact
Blue	Wisdom: Control, Calm, Silent, Thinker, Planner
Purple	Peace: Benign, Reassured, Enlightened, Empathetic
Black	Balanced: Self Mastery, Self-Control, Awareness

WEAKNESSES

White (Devoid): The weakness of a white blackguard lies in their corrupted mind, which becomes empty and indifferent. They may struggle to form meaningful connections with others or feel empathy. Their apathetic nature can make them vulnerable to manipulation or isolation, as they lack the emotional depth and passion necessary to defend themselves.

Red (Passionate): The weakness of a red blackguard stems from their intense emotions, such as anger, disdain, vindictiveness, and hatred. Their fiery temper and inability to control their emotions can lead to impulsive and reckless actions. Their passionate nature may blind them to reason and logic, making them susceptible to manipulation through emotional manipulation or provocation.

Orange (Lust): The weakness of an orange blackguard lies in their insatiable desires, including greed, aggression, and anxiousness. Their constant pursuit of pleasure and material gain can make them vulnerable to temptation and exploitation. Their excessive ambition and restlessness can lead them to make impulsive decisions, leaving them exposed to manipulation or unforeseen consequences.

Yellow (Pride): The weakness of a yellow blackguard is rooted in their overwhelming pride, which manifests as ambition, belligerence, and bipolar behavior. Their unyielding sense of self-importance can blind them to their own limitations and make them susceptible to arrogance. Their prideful nature may lead them to overlook crucial details or underestimate their opponents, making them vulnerable to exploitation or strategic manipulation.

Green (Happy): The weakness of a green blackguard stems from their naivety and trustfulness. Their inherently hopeful and willing nature can make them vulnerable to manipulation and deception. Their emphasis on maintaining harmony and positive relationships may lead them to underestimate the darker motives of others, leaving them exposed to betrayal or strategic exploitation.

Blue (Wisdom): The weakness of a blue blackguard lies in their constant pursuit of control, calmness, and silence. Their desire for order and understanding may make them vulnerable to overthinking or analysis paralysis. Their preference for careful planning and reliance on logic can be exploited by those who are adept at manipulating their thoughts or emotions.

Purple (Peace): The weakness of a purple blackguard stems from their benign and empathetic nature. Their desire for peace and enlightenment can make them susceptible to manipulation through appeals to their compassion. Their inclination to see the good in others and trust their intentions may blind them to potential threats or ulterior motives.

Black (Balanced): Although black blackguards possess self-mastery, self-control, and awareness, their weakness lies in their susceptibility to overconfidence. Their balanced nature may lead them to underestimate the abilities of others or become complacent in their own skills. This overconfidence can be exploited by opponents who are adept at finding vulnerabilities or exploiting weaknesses.

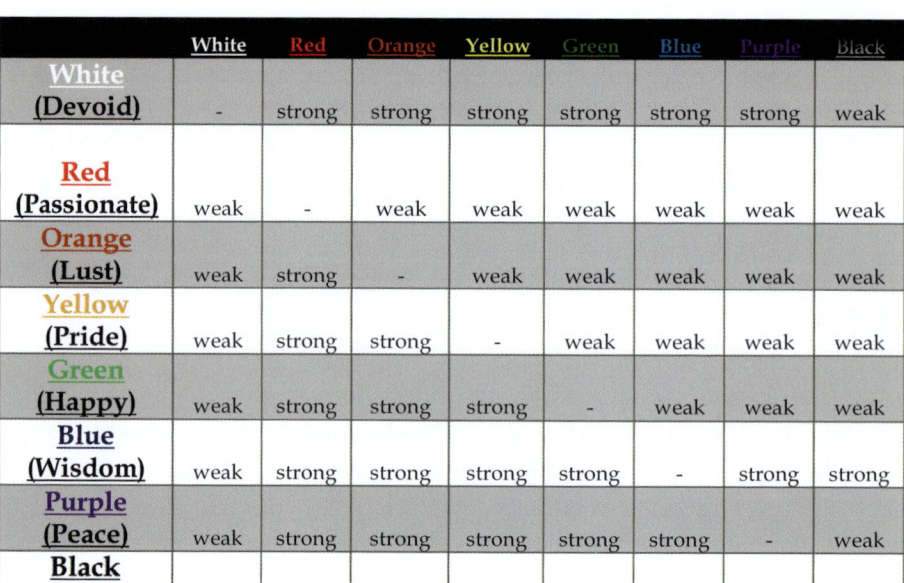

	White	Red	Orange	Yellow	Green	Blue	Purple	Black
White (Devoid)	-	strong	strong	strong	strong	strong	strong	weak
Red (Passionate)	weak	-	weak	weak	weak	weak	weak	weak
Orange (Lust)	weak	strong	-	weak	weak	weak	weak	weak
Yellow (Pride)	weak	strong	strong	-	weak	weak	weak	weak
Green (Happy)	weak	strong	strong	strong	-	weak	weak	weak
Blue (Wisdom)	weak	strong	strong	strong	strong	-	strong	strong
Purple (Peace)	weak	strong	strong	strong	strong	strong	-	weak
Black (Balanced)	strong	strong	strong	strong	strong	weak	strong	-

White is strong against Red, Orange, Yellow, Green, Blue, and Purple, but weak against Black. Corrupted boko grants unparalleled and uncontrollable strength over the forces.

Red is weak against Orange, Yellow, Green, Blue, Purple, and Black. More focused and balanced colors can easily manipulate or overcome their intense but uncontrolled emotions.

Orange is weak against Yellow, Green, Blue, Purple, and Black. The wisdom and self-control of other colors can temper their desires and aggression.

Yellow is weak against Green, Blue, Purple, and Black. The strengths of other colors can be exploited or balance their pride and playful nature.

Green is weak against Blue, Purple, and Black. More strategic and insightful colors can take its naivety and trustfulness advantage of.

Blue is strong against Green, Purple, and Black. Its wisdom, control, and understanding allow it to outmaneuver and counteract the vulnerabilities of these colors.

Purple is weak against Blue and Black. Its peaceful and empathetic nature may struggle against the strategic thinking and self-control of these colors.

Black is strong against White, Red, Orange, Yellow, Green, Purple, but weak against Blue. Its balanced and self-mastery nature allows it to counteract the weaknesses of most other colors, but the strategic thinking of Blue can challenge its advantages.

It's important to note that these relationships are not absolute, and the outcome of conflicts between colors may depend on various factors, such as the skill, experience, and specific circumstances of the individuals involved.

SOL GALNESE SEASONS & MONTHS

<u>SEHLIWA - RAIN (106 Days)</u>:

Sehliwa is the first season of the calendar, lasting for three months. It represents the period of abundant rainfall and nourishment for the land. During Sehliwa, the skies open, and the region experiences frequent showers and thunderstorms. The rains bring relief from the scorching heat and rejuvenate the flora and fauna. Rivers and lakes overflow with water, ensuring an ample supply for agriculture and sustaining wildlife. Farmers seize this opportunity to sow their crops and take advantage of the fertile soil. Sehliwa is associated with growth, fertility, and the beginning of the natural cycle. Since Sehliwa lasts for 106 days and is divided into three months.

Maravi (35 days) Tuvimba (35 days) Lumina (36 days)

<u>SEHHA - GROWTH (136 Days)</u>:
Following Sehliwa, Sehha marks the second season and spans five months. This phase represents a period of growth and prosperity. The rainfall from Sehliwa provides the moisture for the plants to flourish, resulting in lush vegetation and blooming flowers. The landscape transforms into a vibrant tapestry of colors, and the scent of blossoms fills the air. Farmers tend to their crops, witnessing their hard work come to fruition. The abundance of food and resources allows communities to thrive and engage in various activities. Sehha is a time of energy, progress, and development. Sehha spans 136 days and is spread across five months.

Ashadia (27 days) Zephyria (27 days) Floriana (27 days) Verdanta (27 days) Solara (28 days)

SEHFO - DROUGHT (118 Days):

Sehfo, the final season, encompasses four months and signifies a period of drought and scarcity. The rains of Sehliwa gradually diminish, and the land experiences dryness and aridity. The scorching sun dominates the sky, causing water sources to dwindle and vegetation to wither. The absence of rain poses challenges for agriculture and forces communities to conserve resources. Wildlife adapts to the harsh conditions, seeking shelter and conserving energy. During Sehfo, people rely on stored food and carefully manage their water supplies. It is a time of resilience, endurance, and strategic planning to navigate through the scarcity. Sehfo encompasses a total of 118 days and is divided into four months.

Embera (30 days) Aridora (29 days) Serelia (30 days) Scorcha (29 days)

THE ZUHARA CURRENCY SYSTEM

COPPER	BRONZE	SILVER	GOLD	ZUHARA
10	1			
100	10			
1000	100	1		
10000	1000	10	1	
100000	10000	100	10	1

Copper: The lowest denomination in the currency system. It represents the basic unit of value and is commonly used for small transactions or everyday purchases. For example, a copper coin has the same value as a small food item.

Bronze: This is a step up from copper and represents a slightly higher denomination. Bronze coins are worth 10 times the value of a copper coin. They are used for transactions that exceed the value of a single copper unit but are still relatively small.

Silver: The next level in the currency hierarchy, silver represents a significant increase in value. It is a more valuable metal, and silver coins are typically used for larger transactions. One silver coin is equivalent to 100 bronze coins, or 1,000 copper coins. It is often used for mid-range purchases, such as clothing, household goods, or larger food items.

Gold: Gold is considered a precious metal, and its inclusion in the currency system signifies a substantial increase in value. Gold coins are worth 10 times the value of a silver coin. They are typically reserved for high-value transactions, such as luxury goods, expensive jewelry, or significant investments.

Zuhara: Zuhara is the highest denomination in this currency progression. It represents the ultimate level of value and is extremely rare and precious. Zuhara coins are worth 10 times the value of a gold coin, or 100 times the value of a silver coin. Zuhara currency is used for transactions involving luxury assets, high-end investments, or exceptionally valuable goods.

THE DIVINE FAMILY OF SEH

Seh - Mother of Creation: Seh is the central figure in this divine family and the creative force and the source of existence. She is the progenitor of all the other gods and embodies the power of creation.

CHILDREN OF SEH

Sehuvu - God of Strength and Violence: As the first son of Seh, Sehuvu represents strength and violence. He embodies raw power and physical prowess, reflecting the primal and intense aspects of existence.

Sehshima - God of Dignity and Integrity: Sehshima, the daughter of Seh, embodies dignity and integrity. She represents moral values, honor, and righteousness, bringing a sense of virtue to the divine family.

Sehoja - God of Unity and Fertility: Sehoja, the second son of Seh, symbolizes unity and fertility. He fosters harmony and cooperation among beings while also embodying the power of fertility and growth in the natural world.

GRANDCHILDREN OF SEH

Seheupe - God of Corruption: Seheupe, the first son of Sehuvu and associated with the color White, is the god of corruption. He is a darker aspect of existence, where purity is tainted and twisted, and has dominion over the Cesspool.

Sehkundu - God of Passion: Sehkundu, the second son of Sehuvu and associated with Red, represents passion. He embodies intense emotions, including anger, desire, and a fiery disposition.

Sehgwa - God of Desire: Sehgwa, the daughter of Sehuvu and associated with Orange, is the god of desire. She personifies longing, craving, and the pursuit of gratification.

Sehjamo - God of Indulgence: Sehjamo, the son of Sehshima and associated with Yellow, represents indulgence. He embodies the pursuit of pleasure, excess, and self-gratification.

Sehjami - God of Adroitness: Sehjami, the first daughter of Sehshima and associated with Green, is the god of adroitness. She represents skill, agility, and dexterity, reflecting a keenness and proficiency in various endeavors.

Sehluu - God of Wisdom: Sehluu, the second daughter of Sehshima and associated with Blue, is the god of wisdom. She embodies deep insight, knowledge, and intellectual acumen.

Sehbarau - God of Tranquility: Sehbarau, the son of Sehoja and associated with the color Purple, represents tranquility. He embodies peace, serenity, and a sense of calmness.

Seheusi - God of Purity: Seheusi, the daughter of Sehoja and associated with the color Black, is the god of purity. She symbolizes cleanliness, innocence, and the absence of corruption.

ABOUT THE AUTHOR

I am Raymond Singclare Cobb, an independent author from Compton, California. A creative powerhouse, I craft mind-blowing worlds that'll leave you utterly spellbound! Buckle up for epic journeys across fantasy, sci-fi, and horror.

With a bachelor's degree in creative writing from Full Sail University, my storytelling skills are finely tuned. My books are packed with unforgettable characters and extraordinary experiences that'll sweep you off your feet.

But it doesn't stop with books! I am also a dedicated father, sharing my love for storytelling with my children, igniting their imaginations for generations to come.

Already fifteen books deep, I'm always on the hunt for new horizons to captivate readers like you. Imagination is my superpower, and I invite publishers, magazines, and editors to join me on this thrilling journey.

Get ready for an adventure with no limits! Follow me on social media **@mindtheytypos** and check out www.rscobb.com for all the latest updates and news. Let's shape new worlds together with every stroke of the pen!

BOOKS BY R.S COBB

TALES FROM THE OTHER SIDE SERIES

One

The Téreta

Instantaneous

Conjured 2020

Escape

STAND-ALONE TITLES

Chrononaut

Complacency Leads to Government Control

Live, Laugh, Learn: Studying a Semester in London

POETRY COLLECTIONS

Flawed King

In the Hall of Mirrors

Reckless Wordplay

COMPILATIONS

Some Stories I Wrote

A Simulation for Assimilation

BLACKGUARD SERIES

Way of the Askari

Prelude to Blackguard: Echoes of Defiance

Thank you for choosing my book!

Welcome to your gateway to captivating literature. I specialize in fantasy, science fiction, thrillers, and poetry, offering high-quality reads across diverse genres.

Unlock special offers, bonus content, and stay updated on new releases at
www.rscobb.com

Printed in Dunstable, United Kingdom

74944080R00033